MR. CLEVER

by Roger Hargreaves

EGMONT WORLD LIMITED.

Mr Clever was quite the cleverest person ever.

The Cleverest Person In The World!

And, he knew it!

"Oh, I am so very very CLEVER," he used to say.

To himself more often than not.

He lived in Cleverland where, as you may know, everybody and everything is as clever as can be.

In Cleverland clever trees manage to grow apples and oranges at the same time!

In Cleverland clever flowers get up and go for a walk!

Clever worms drive around in cars all day!

And clever elephants play tennis!

Oh yes, Cleverland is quite the most clever place.

Would you like to live there?

Mr Clever does.

"Oh, I am so very very CLEVER to build such a clever house," he used to go around telling everybody.

One morning, Mr Clever was awakened by his special Mr Clever alarm clock.

Not only did it wake you up by ringing a bell: it also switched on a light; and said "Good morning"; and made a cup of tea; and showed what the weather was going to be; and told you the time; and showed you the date. It also whistled cheerfully while it was doing all that!

Mr Clever yawned, got up, washed, cleaned his teeth (with his special Mr Clever toothbrush which squeezed toothpaste on to the brush out of the handle), and went downstairs for breakfast.

He popped a slice of bread into his special Mr Clever electric toaster.

Which not only toasted the bread, but also spread it with butter and marmalade, AND cut off the crusts!

After breakfast he went for a long walk.

An extremely long walk.

In fact, such a long walk that he walked all the way out of Cleverland, although he didn't know it.

He met somebody who was also out for a walk.

Do you know who it was?

That's right.

Mr Happy!

"Hello," cried Mr Clever. "I'm The Cleverest Person In The World!"

"Oh good," said Mr Happy. "Then you must be clever enough to make up a really good joke to tell me."

He laughed.

"Jokes make me happy," he explained.

Mr Clever's face fell.

"I don't know any jokes," he admitted.

"Well, that's not very clever of you, is it?" said Mr Happy, and went off.

Mr Clever went on.

And do you know who he met next?

That's right.

Mr Greedy!

"Hello," cried Mr Clever. "I'm The Cleverest Person In The World!"

"Oh good," said Mr Greedy. "Then you can tell me the recipe of the world's most delicious dish."

He licked his lips.

"I like food," he explained.

Mr Clever's face fell.

"I can't cook," he admitted. "And I don't know any recipes!"

"Well, that's not very clever of you, is it?" said Mr Greedy, and went off.

In search of food.

Mr Clever went on.

And who do you think he met next?

Yes.

Mr Forgetful!

"Hello," cried Mr Clever. "I'm The Cleverest Person In The World!"

"Oh good," said Mr Forgetful. "Then you can tell me what my name is."

He smiled apologetically.

"I've forgotten," he explained.

Mr Clever's face fell for the third time that morning.

"But I don't know your name," he admitted. "We've only just met!"

"Well, that's not very clever of you, is it?" said Mr Forgetful, and he too went off.

Forgetting to say goodbye!

And so it went on. All day.

Mr Clever couldn't tell Mr Sneeze the cure for a cold.

And he couldn't tell Mr Small how he could grow bigger.

And he couldn't tell Mr Jelly what the secret of being brave was.

And he couldn't tell Mr Topsy-Turvy how to talk the round way right.

I mean the right way round.

A not very clever day!

Not at all.

Not a bit.

As by now he wasn't feeling anything like The Cleverest Person In The World, Mr Clever decided he'd better go home.

He passed a pair of worms who were having a chat.

"Who's that?" asked one worm.

"That," replied the other worm, "is Mr Clever, The Cleverest Person In The World, on his way home to Cleverland!"

The first worm thought.

"He can't be that clever," he replied . . .

. . . "he's going the wrong way!"

3 Great Offers For Mr Men Fans

1 Token
EGMONT WORLD

1 FREE Door Hangers and Posters

In every Mr Men and Little Miss Book like this one you will find a special token. Collect 6 and we will send you either a brilliant Mr. Men or Little Miss poster and a Mr Men or Little Miss double sided, full colour, bedroom door hanger. Apply using the coupon overleaf, enclosing six tokens and a 50p coin for your choice of two items.

Egmont World tokens can be used towards any other Egmont World / World International token scheme promotions, in early learning and story / activity books.

Posters: Tick your preferred choice of either Mr Men ☐ or Little Miss ☐

Door Hangers: Choose from: Mr. Nosey & Mr Muddle ☐, Mr Greedy & Mr Lazy ☐, Mr Tickle & Mr Grumpy ☐, Mr Slow & Mr Busy ☐, Mr Messy & Mr Quiet ☐, Mr Perfect & Mr Forgetful ☐, Little Miss Fun & Little Miss Late ☐, Little Miss Helpful & Little Miss Tidy ☐, Little Miss Busy & Little Miss Brainy ☐, Little Miss Star & Little Miss Fun ☐. (Please tick)

ENTRANCE FEE 3 SAUSAGES
MR. GREEDY

2 Mr Men Library Boxes

Keep your growing collection of Mr Men and Little Miss books in these superb library boxes. With an integral carrying handle and stay-closed fastener, these full colour, plastic boxes are fantastic. They are just £5.49 each including postage. Order overleaf.

3 Join The Club

To join the fantastic Mr Men & Little Miss Club, check out the page overleaf NOW!

MR MEN and LITTLE MISS™ & © 1998 Mrs. Roger Hargreaves

• RETURN THIS WHOLE PAGE •

Join Our Club!

MR. MEN & Little Miss CLUB

When you become a member of the fantastic Mr Men and Little Miss Club you'll receive a personal letter from Mr Happy and Little Miss Giggles, a club badge with your name, and a superb Welcome Pack (pictured below right).

You'll also get birthday and Christmas cards from the Mr Men and Little Misses, 2 newsletters crammed with special offers, privileges and news, and a copy of the 12 page Mr Men catalogue which includes great party ideas.

If it were on sale in the shops, the Welcome Pack alone might cost around £13. But a year's membership is just £9.99 (plus 73p postage) with a 14 day money-back guarantee if you are not delighted!

HOW TO APPLY To apply for any of these three great offers, ask an adult to complete the coupon below and send it with appropriate payment and tokens (where required) to: Mr Men Offers, PO Box 7, Manchester M19 2HD. Credit card orders for Club membership ONLY by telephone, please call: 01403 242727.

To be completed by an adult

❏ **1.** Please send a poster and door hanger as selected overleaf. I enclose six tokens and a 50p coin for post (coin not required if you are also taking up 2. or 3. below).

❏ **2.** Please send ___ Mr Men Library case(s) and ___ Little Miss Library case(s) at £5.49 each.

❏ **3.** Please enrol the following in the Mr Men & Little Miss Club at £10.72 (inc postage)

Fan's Name:_____Fan's Address:_____

_____Post Code:_____Date of birth:___ /___ /___

Your Name:_____Your Address:_____

Post Code:_____Name of parent or guardian (if not you):_____

Total amount due: £_____ (£5.49 per Library Case, £10.72 per Club membership)

❏ I enclose a cheque or postal order payable to Egmont World Limited.

❏ Please charge my MasterCard / Visa account.

Card number:

Expiry Date: _____ /_____   Signature: _____